We've all felt the same way at some point in our lives. There has been that niggling thought in the back of our minds that there's got to be something better out there. Something better than the mundane day in day out tasks that we set ourselves. Something much more worthwhile, that we could do with our lives. A life where we could follow our dreams and finally enjoy the things we spend our time doing.

Jack Somerfield has been given the chance to make that leap and he's determined to grasp at it with both hands, no matter what the consequences are.

In this debut release from Liane Hoare, **The Ghost Writer** is a tale that will grip you from the very first, right up to the last chapter.

This is a moving story about a young man that we can all relate to, who has some incredible aspirations of what he wants to do with his life.

The Ghost Writer is a twisty tale that will keep you guessing right up until the end. It will make you want to go back and read it again to try and pick out any clues along the way.

Also by Liane Hoare and available from www.lulu.com

THE FORENSIC KILLER
A BOOK OF POETRY

Other titles coming soon from Liane Hoare

SIX MONTHS LATER
THE APP
CURSE OF THE FAIRGROUND
THE NETWORK
THE BLACK DOG

About the Author

Liane Hoare lives in Surrey, United Kingdom with her partner, Daniel Pelling. Liane has been writing poetry and short stories since she was nine years old after much encouragement from her Grandmother, June Checkley. After she passed away, Liane made a promise to work towards what her Gran always believed she could do to honour her memory. In her spare time, Liane also enjoys taking photos and writing movie reviews. You can find her blog at http://lianehoarephotography.wordpress.com

LIANE HOARE THE GHOST WRITER

www.lulu.com

Copyright © 2011 by Liane Hoare
First published in Great Britain in 2010
by Lulu Enterprises UK Ltd

Hoare, Liane, 1982 -
The Ghost Writer
2nd Edition

ISBN 978-1-4478-1386-6

Printed and bound in Great Britain by www.lulu.com, a division of Lulu Enterprises UK Ltd, Barking is Fortis House, 160 London Road, Barking, IG11 8BB.

Front cover photo © Liane Hoare Photography
Photo edited by Samuel Pelling

This book is dedicated to my family and friends who have believed in me from the beginning. I would like to show my appreciation to my partner, Daniel Pelling, for standing by me and helping me to unlock my true ability.
My heartfelt gratitude will always lay with my Gran, June Checkley, who is missed everyday. Everything I do is in memory to her.

Sincerely,
LH

Chapter One

It's not enough. It's never been enough and as the hands of time ticked away, he wondered why there wasn't more to his seemingly mundane life. More than the stresses and worries that life had to offer him. More than the monotonous shirts and ties. More than the boring, dead end job he struggled to face going to everyday. More than the endless meetings and cackling of his co-workers selling useless tat to poor little old ladies that didn't know better. The incessant hum of the life he so desperately longed for was buzzing in his ears. Or perhaps it was the sound of his phone vibrating on the dashboard of his car while his boss was calling him for the tenth time that morning. Whatever it was, Jack Somerfield was reaching an all time low and the disenchantment had gripped him, refusing to let go.

"There has got to be something more to life, surely," thought Jack as he sat at his desk in The City, holding his head in his hands, sighing.

The grey hairs were showing through again after he'd pulled them out of his head that morning. With the amount he was pulling out each day, he wondered if he would be bald by the time he turned 30. He always knew that there was something missing and something greater that he was destined for besides the usual day in, day out stresses of living and working in Central London. Besides these usual woes he was missing his girlfriend more than ever.

They had met three years earlier while Jack was on business in Canada and instantly fell in love. It was hard on them being away from each other but Jack had aspirations of packing up his high-stress job in London to emigrate to Canada to be with her. Lisa was in her mid-twenties and worked as a Highway Patrol Officer. She was living at her brother, Archie's apartment until Jack could move out there and they could get their own home together. When she met Jack, she worked at a bar close to where he was staying. It was almost as though fate had brought them together. Lisa would always tell him that his deep, blue eyes were what first attracted him to her. The night they met he was sitting in the corner of the bar alone. He looked sad and lonely so she introduced herself to him. Jack was very shy at first but warmed up quickly as they got to know each other through the course of the evening. He told her everything about his life. Something struck him about Lisa. He felt he could tell her anything and she wouldn't mind. Perhaps she was just doing her job at the time and trying to get him to buy another drink but when they got talking it felt as though they had known each other for years.

The memories Jack was having about that month he was out there for came flooding back to him. They made him happy and took his mind of the impending doom that came with sitting at his desk.
As well as his day job, Jack had been ghost writing on the side to help fund his future aspirations and when the day would finally arrive he thought that it would be the chance to make something of his life, and to have a real chance to show the world what he was capable of. The trouble with Jack was that he was terrified of screwing up, which is why he would ghost write for other people or publish novels under a pseudonym so no-one would ever think he was a failure. He didn't believe enough in himself. His close friends and family would tell him that he was really good, but he just couldn't see it. He refused to believe it. At 29 years old, Jack was scared of taking chances. Don't get him wrong. He loved what he wrote about and was proud of it but the fear of rejection was just too much for him to take. He felt like a ghost at work most of the time and was always passed by for any promotions. Jack was extremely downhearted about the direction his life was taking. He learnt not to ask for anything anymore. Though he would slog his guts off in his

job and do any overtime that was asked for him, he was always told that everything he did wasn't good enough. Jack dreaded his appraisals with his boss, whom he had nicknamed the Spawn of Satan, as they would always turn into a good excuse for him to pick holes in every little thing he did. Any task he was given, the Spawn of Satan would find fault in it.

Chapter Two

Another week of hell had passed and it was almost the weekend. Though most Fridays were just like any other day, this day was different. Jack had got a call to say that his visa application had been approved. He was now beginning to see light at the end of a very long, dark tunnel. He couldn't wait to tell Lisa the good news, but with the five-hour time difference he knew he couldn't call her, as she would be sleeping.

After the long and tiresome journey to work, Jack hurried up to the open plan office on the third floor and sat down at his desk. He logged onto his computer instantly as he couldn't wait to email Lisa to tell her the good news, although typing out his resignation letter to give to his boss would be somewhat more satisfying. He smiled to himself at the thought of Lisa opening her emails later that day and reading the one he was about to send. As he was typing away he was grinning like a Cheshire cat about everything. The thought of telling his boss where to stick his lousy job was getting his adrenaline pumping. After he'd finished typing his letter he printed off a copy and signed it before putting it in an envelope. Marching over to his boss' office he had a sense of excitement in every step he took. He didn't care about the strange looks people were giving him as he almost skipped joyfully to the uninviting, wooden door. Jack used to hate going to his boss' office, as going through the door felt like stepping through the gates of hell, especially the mornings when he would be given mammoth and impossible tasks to do. Despite this, he would still knuckle down and get on with things. Every time someone left the company, he would envy them and wish he could take their place. Now he was getting his wishes. Everything was falling into place. None of Jack's colleagues knew he was a ghostwriter on the side. He had once caught sight of one of the receptionists reading one of his books, though he wouldn't dare tell them that it he had written it. Not that anyone would believe he was capable of doing something so creative anyway. He was such a shy and withdrawn individual at times. After all, if he didn't believe in himself, why would anyone else?

As he got ever closer to stepping through the door that would eventually change his life forever, he had a sudden sense of relief wash over him like waves on a beach. The feeling was incredible and he couldn't wait to hand his letter of resignation over to his boss.

Tim Jacobs was the same age as Jack. They had gone to the same school and he always thought that Tim looked down upon him. Even then Tim would bully him and steal his lunch money everyday. Just goes to show things never change. His appearance was bully like too, with his heavy-set build and bald head, he looked like he belonged in one of those street gangs you see causing riots at football matches and things. Not what you would expect to be in charge of a multi-million pound company.

Although Tim doesn't steal Jack's lunch money anymore, in the three years he had been at the company, Tim had refused to give him a pay rise. Taking away that one thing away he craved, a chance to make something of his life. In the beginning Jack was looking into self-publishing, but because Tim wouldn't give him that well-deserved pay rise, he had to explore other options. It was then he turned to ghost writing and after his first piece was published, he used the money to apply for the visa he so desperately wanted. Lisa was always very encouraging of him and suggested him to a friend of her brother.

Billy Johnson was a young publisher living in Canada. He had set up his own publishing company called OzCorp after he'd won the lottery while living in his native Australia. Once he'd established a reasonable client list he upped sticks and emigrated to give the young writers of America and Canada a chance to kick start their career. When Lisa showed Archie one of Jack's stories, he suggested sending it to Billy. The instant Billy read it he begged Lisa for Jack's email address. Billy always endeavoured to give people chances and he saw potential in Jack. Of course there was room for improvement, but he believed in Jack enough to publish his first pseudonym-written work. Billy had always insisted on getting Jack's own name put on the cover, but knew he would be fighting a losing battle in trying to convince him otherwise.

Jack reached Tim's office and knocked on the newly varnished door. It was now so shiny that Jack could see his reflection in the paintwork.

Tim called from inside, giving Jack permission to step inside, "Enter!"

Jack opened the door and stepped inside.

"Hi Tim," he said, "I thought I would stop by and give you this personally," as he handed over the envelope.

"What's this?" questioned Tim, tearing open the envelope.

"My letter of resignation," explained Jack, "I'm moving to Canada. My visa application has been approved."

"I didn't even know you had applied for one," queried Tim, "Funny how I'm always the last to know about what goes on in your mediocre life."

"Since when did you care what goes on in my life?" snapped Jack.

"I don't," said Tim sarcastically, "I was making a point."

"I figured that much was true," sighed Jack, "I would say it has been nice working for you. But I'd be lying if I did."
Tim discarded the envelope in the bin and filed the letter away without reading it.

"Well it wouldn't be hard to replace you anyway," he said, "Just don't expect me to give you any references."

"I wasn't asking for any," Jack replied, slightly antagonised as he went to go back out to the open plan office.

"Don't let the door hit you on the way out, Jack," said Tim as the door slammed behind Jack.

"Is everything okay?" asked Jason, one of Jack's colleagues.

Jack smiled and said, "It is now. I'm out of here in two weeks!"

"Oh, he didn't fire you did he?" asked a concerned Jason.

"No," replied Jack excitedly, "I just handed in my resignation. I'm emigrating to Canada and I can't wait!"

"Wow that's excellent!" said a more relaxed Jason, "I'm really happy for you!"

"Thanks," grinned Jack, "Listen, I'm not expecting many people to turn up, but I feel a celebration is in order on my last day."

"Most definitely!" said Jason, rubbing his hands together, "Leave that with me."

"Excellent," smiled Jack, "Anyway, I guess I should at least do some work today," as he walked away back to his desk.

Jason Webber had been with the company just over a year. He was six years younger than Jack and it was his first job since finishing university. Jack had taken Jason under his wing to start with but as the months went on, Jason found his feet and quickly became an established member of the team.

Chapter Three

It was Jack's last day working in the company that he liked to refer to as hell. He once told Lisa that some mornings he dreaded going into work, as he wasn't looking forward to whatever was waiting for him when he got there. Now he didn't have to worry about that anymore. Once the end of the day came around he would be let out and his sentence would be over. He would no longer be a number, he would be a free man.

All morning, Jack was revelling in the excitement at leaving. There wasn't a thank you presentation from Tim, nor a leaving card or collection. He didn't care though. He would much rather slip out unnoticed and disappear without a trace from that wretched company and away from Tim's iron-fist clutch.

"Not long now," commented Jason from his desk opposite Jack.

Jack smiled and said, "Nope. I am literally counting down the minutes now."

"That'll take longer," laughed Jason, "Try hours instead."

"Good idea. Glad someone around here as a brain," Jack laughed back.

"Ssssh," hushed Jason, "Don't say that too loudly incase Tim hears you. If he thinks I have a brain he'll task me with more mind-numbing projects. Especially as he hasn't got you to palm them off to anymore."

"I'm sorry," said Jack, "I really feel for you if he does. After all, I've spent the last three years dealing with his crap so know exactly what you would be going through."

"I know you have," insisted Jason, "We all felt like telling him he was an ass for giving you so much shtick. But at least you're getting out of it now."

"Hell yeah!" laughed Jack.

An hour later Tim came out of hiding from his office and walked over to Jack's desk with some forms in his hand, slamming them down in front of him.

"Make sure you fill these in before you leave today," said Tim without any emotion before walking away again as quickly as he came over.

Jack read through the forms before attempting to fill them in between the phone ringing and his colleagues coming over to congratulate him on it being his last day. They were questionnaires about his experience with the company and to ensure that all items belonging to them would be returned, with the completed forms, to the office administration team. He was honest with his answers, especially about Tim. Why should he lie? He had nothing to lose and everything to gain as soon as he stepped out of that door for the final time. After all, what would Tim do, fire him? He went back to watching the clock and realised that time didn't appear to be ticking away. Were the minutes moving that slowly, or did the battery need changing? Either way, he couldn't wait to get out of there.

It was lunchtime and Jason was badgering Jack to veer away from his desk.

"Come on, Jack," said Jason impatiently, "Time for some lunchtime beers!"

"Okay, okay!" laughed Jack, "You don't need to tell me twice," before he stood up and put his jacket on.

"There should be time for a game of pool as well, I'd imagine. Let's see if I can't beat you one last time before you jet off to pastures new," joked Jason.

"Ha! Beat me? Since when has that ever happened?" laughed Jack.

Jason smiled, "Well, there's a first time for everything, surely?" he said.

They headed out the door and got in Jason's car. For the last couple of days he had been acting as Jack's chauffer since he had sold his car. Jack's flat was practically empty as well, except for the small amount he was taking with him.

"Are we going to the Prince of Wales?" asked Jason.

"Of course," replied Jack, before they drove off.

It was finally here. The end of Jack's sentence had at last arrived. He was beginning to think the day would never be over, as it seemed to have dragged on and on. He had done his round of goodbyes to the people who actually cared that he was leaving. No one else seemed bothered that he was even going. He wondered if they would even notice that he wasn't sat at his desk anymore.

Jack often had that feeling. Wondering what it would be like if he wasn't there anymore and wondering if they would even know. Now he could wonder no more, he was one of the lucky ones that he used to envy when they left the company. Now it was his turn.

Jack headed down to the car park with Jason once he had handed everything back to the office administrator.

"There's no going back now," said Jason as they got to his car.

"I wouldn't want to," smiled Jack before looking up at Tim's office window.

He saw Tim standing there watching him, almost as though he was making sure Jack was leaving.

Jack was free. Free from the stresses and worries. Free to start the rest of his life with Lisa. Free to enjoy the new experiences he will face in Canada. Free to be the man he has always wanted to be.

Chapter Four

Jack and Lisa were in their new home by Lake Erie in Ontario. Jack had been living in Canada for just over a month now and was feeling more relaxed in life than he has ever felt before. The blizzard that had been keeping them housebound for the last week or so had finally stopped. There was in-depth coverage all over the news stations about the approaching snowstorm in the week leading up to it, causing pandemonium in the stores. Swarms of people sweeping through, grabbing whatever they could lay their hands on, panic buying and stocking up on the essentials in case they got snowed in. By the time Jack and Lisa could get round to doing it, half the shelves were bare. They didn't care however, as they had each other. The weekend before the blizzard came, Jack and Lisa were out shopping in Wainfleet when they walked by a quaint, little jewellery store. They hadn't discussed getting engaged before that day but Jack always knew Lisa wanted to. He wasn't quite ready to take that step, but he was happy to stand with her as she admired the rings in the window. There was one ring in particular that caught her eye. It reminded her of one that her grandmother used to have when she was young. The memories made her smile as Jack put his arms around her and vowed that one day he would get her a ring just like it when the time was right.

Jack came into the living room with two hot, steaming mugs of cocoa. He sat down on the sofa next to Lisa and handed her a mug as he put his down on the coffee table beside him. Lisa put her feet up and leant back against Jack's chest, curling up in front of the roaring log fire that was keeping them warm and safe from the freezing temperatures outside.

"I am so glad we did this," said Jack as he sat running his fingers through Lisa's long, blonde hair, "I couldn't be happier."

Lisa smiled and said, "So am I, having you here makes my life feel complete."

"It looks as though the blizzard is finally coming to an end," commented Jack as he looked out of the window.

"Thank god for that!" replied Lisa gleefully, "Then I can get back out to work again. I can only imagine what mess will need to be cleared up when we get back out on the road."

With Lisa's job it meant she worked long hours and had to deal with all sorts of things whilst out on Patrol. There was no telling what would be waiting for her when she got back to work. Jack felt really bad that Lisa's job was the sole income for them both but she always insisted that he stayed home and concentrated on his writing, as that is where his heart truly lies. Apart from Lisa, writing was his life and he was good at it when he truly put his mind to it.

The following morning the snow had almost gone. Lisa was getting ready to head off to work. Jack was already up and sat in front of his laptop, waiting for some inspiration to come to him. It had been a struggle for him to come up with any ideas since moving. The stress of the emigration took it out of him. Lisa walked into the study and put her hands on his shoulders. He looked up at her and smiled.

"I always thought you looked good in that uniform," said Jack.

"Think of it as your inspiration," she smiled.

He grinned and said, "If I think of that I'll be thinking of something else."

"On that note I should go else I'll be late," laughed Lisa.

He grabbed hold of her hand and said, "Can't you stay a little longer?"

"I wish I could," she sighed, "But I really will be late if I don't go now."

"Okay then, sweetheart," he replied, "Can't wait to see you later."

"Me too," she smiled sweetly before kissing him goodbye, "I love you."

"I love you too," he said as she headed out the door to her Patrol Car.

Jack sat back in his chair and put his hands on his head, sighing. His dark head of hair had hints of grey in it. Clearly he was still stressed about something. His mind was blank for ideas. He had writers block and it was making him depressed. He got up and walked around the house as he tried to come up with ideas. His mind was elsewhere. All he kept thinking about was how badly he wanted to be successful, and it was that which was stopping him from coming up with any good ideas. Pacing up and down the hallway was about all he could manage at the moment. He was feeling numb and it wasn't comfortable.

Two hours had passed and Jack still hadn't managed to write anything. He sat forward in his chair, staring at the curser flickering on the screen of his laptop. Running his finger along the mouse pad to the Start menu, he wondered if he should play Solitaire for the umpteenth time today. He gazed over to the corner of the study at his guitar. The strings were glistening from the sunlight beaming on them through the window, begging to be played. He got up off his chair and walked over to pick up his guitar. The sleek, blue Ashton needed re-tuning but when it did, it sounded beautiful. Jack was in no way the greatest guitar player in the world, but when he needed inspiration, the feeling he got from playing it was magical. Since arriving in Canada, Lisa's brother Archie would go over on a Sunday with his guitar and they would jam together. They'd often spend long afternoons chatting and joking that perhaps they should start a band together if Jack's writing didn't take off.

All of a sudden, it hit him, like a bolt of lightning. He smiled to himself as he put his guitar back down and ran back to his laptop. Sitting down, he cracked his knuckles and began typing away.

After an hour he had already written two chapters. His creative juices were really flowing and he was excited about this possibly being the one that makes him a household name. He was happy with his results and thought to himself that he would even pen his own name on there this time. He phoned Billy at OzCorp and told him about his new project.

"That sounds fantastic!" said Billy with a hint of excitement in his voice, "Does this mean you'll finally put your own name on there?"

Jack laughed and said, "Yeah, I think so. For the first time I'm actually feeling confident about this."

"Good," enthused Billy, "It's about bloody time!"

Billy always believed in Jack and loved the sound of his new novel; he just knew it would be the making of Jack. His other novels that were published under the pseudonym of Jack Russell were good but they missed that gritty edge that most horror novels have. Jack always aspired to be as successful as his hero in the crazy world of horror writing. He had every one of his books and had read them all at least twice. He hoped he could one day be as good as him. For once in his life, Jack was pleased with what he was writing.

By the time Lisa came home Jack was still on fire. He hadn't stopped writing since getting off the phone with Billy. She came into the study where he was still typing away and smiled.

"How's it going?" she asked.

Jack stopped and turned around.

"Great!" he said, glowing, "I think I finally have it."

She walked over to him.

"That's brilliant," she said as she put her arms around him, "I'm so happy for you."

"Thanks," he said as he hugged her back, "How was work?"

She sat down on his lap and said, "A bit slow. But it's over and done with so I'm happier now I'm home with you."

Jack smiled and said, "Aw, you're so sweet."

She laughed and said, "Just don't tell anyone."

He laughed back and said, "Don't worry, my love, your secret is safe with me."

Chapter Five

Jack had been writing his new novel, solidly, for five days now. He hadn't been sleeping very much as the ideas kept flowing through his mind, stopping him from being able to switch off. When it comes to horror it takes a lot to scare Jack but as he was reading back over what he had written, it gave him chills. The thought of it scaring potential readers excited him. This was definitely the one for him.

Jack had been awake all night finishing the current chapter he was on. He was so engrossed in it that he hadn't even realised what the time was as Lisa came into the study with a cup of coffee.

"Have you been up all night?" she asked.

"Yeah," he yawned, "I didn't realise what the time was."

"You should get some rest," she insisted, "I'm starting to worry about you."

"Ah, I'll be fine," he replied, "No need to worry about me. I'm as tough as nails," and he gave her a comforting smile.

"Okay then," she replied, "I'll see you tonight."

"See you later," he said as she headed out the door.

Jack sighed and swallowed hard as he heard the front door slam shut behind Lisa. He knew she was right and that he should get some sleep, but he was worried that if he stopped what he was doing then he would lose track; effectively causing him to lose momentum and not get back in 'the zone' again. He needed some fresh air to help clear his mind of these negative thoughts that were now plaguing him. So he went out into the hallway and put on his coat before walking back into the study and taking a sip of his coffee. Jack yawned as he zipped his coat up as far as it will go. He was starting to feel tired now; the lack of sleep was getting to him. Pulling on his fleece lined, thermal beanie hat, he headed out the front door and began walking towards his car. The cold hit him as soon as he stepped outside and when he reached into his coat pocket to get his car keys, he realised he'd left them inside on the table. Not only was the tiredness affecting his mind but also he was becoming grouchy with it and taking it out on Lisa. Feeling really guilty about the whole situation, he wondered how he could make it up to her and to say thank you for standing by him all this time. He went back into the house to pick up his car keys and that's when he knew what he had to do. He grabbed the keys and headed back outside to the bitter cold. The thought of his warm car seemed somewhat inviting. Jack smiled to himself as he climbed inside his 1957 blue Plymouth Fury. Putting on his seatbelt, he started the engine and thrust on the accelerator. The car roared like a lion as the internal combustion caused the petrol to flow through the engine so Jack could head off to town. The Plymouth was Jack's pride and joy. He'd bought the car when he first moved over to Canada out of his first payout from Billy and out of what he had left of the money he used to fund for his big move. He blew the whole lot on her but she was worth it. There are only two things that Jack loved more in life; Lisa and writing, but his car came in as a very close contender. He was yet to come up with a name for her though. She was the closest he could get to the car from one of the novels penned by his hero. Sometimes, when Jack drove her, he would swear she too had a mind of her own. She was a cherry red Fury and although he knew he could never get his hands on one of those, this was the perfect alternative.

Jack pulled out of the drive and headed down the highway to the small town of Wainfleet. It was a twenty-minute drive away from their house near Lake Erie. As Jack was driving he kept thinking about Lisa and when she was admiring the rings in the window of the quaint, little jewellers they had passed a few weeks ago. He had decided that he was now ready to settle down and start a family with her. Life's too short after all. He figured if he could get that ring she had her eye on then that would be a perfect way to make everything up to her.

Jack arrived at the town centre and parked in the multi-storey car park. He was in dire need of some caffeine intake so headed off to the coffee shop for a double espresso first of all. He sat by the window and watched the people passing by. In a way he wished he'd bought his laptop out with him as he was having some good ideas to add to his novel, instead he scrawled them down on a napkin before putting it in his pocket.

Once Jack had finished his coffee, he stood up and headed back out into the cold, crisp air. He took a brisk walk through the town centre, heading straight for the jewellers. He didn't have much money but he endeavoured to find the right ring for Lisa, even if it took him all day.

He arrived outside the jewellers and trawled through the window display for the ring that Lisa had fallen in love with, but to his disappointment, it wasn't there. He opened the door and stepped inside, walking toward the counter.

"Can I help you?" asked the store attendant, Martin.

"Hi there," smiled Jack, "I'm looking for an engagement ring for my girlfriend but not sure what to get her."

Martin nodded and said, "Okay then, do you have any ideas about what she's looking for?"

"Yeah, we were passed here a few weeks ago and you had one in the window that she had her eye on but I couldn't find it just now," said Jack, "It was a gold one, slightly washed out but with diamond encrusted hearts around the band."

Martin thought for a minute.

"Ah yes, I remember the one. Hmm, unfortunately we had a robbery in here a few nights ago," he explained, "The tray that particular ring was on was one of the ones that were stolen."

"Oh no," said Jack, sympathising, "I'm very sorry to hear that."

"Thank you," replied Martin, as he opened the locked drawer under his till and pulled out a small box, placing it on the counter, "Oddly enough, though," while opening the box, "This one was found in this very drawer the next day, and I know for a fact that it was in the same tray that was taken because I checked it myself before closing that night."

It was the same ring Lisa had been admiring.

"Oh my god," said Jack, slightly bemused, "That is very odd. The ring had reminded Lisa of one her grandmother used to wear."

"This ring came to us as an antique from an elderly gentleman a few months ago. We haven't been able to sell it, so if you're still interested it's all yours," suggested Martin.

"A few months ago?" queried Jack, "That was around the time Lisa's grandmother died. Can you remember his name?"

Martin took out his donations book and looked through the log.

"Let's see. Yes, it was a Gerald Smith," he said.

"Are you serious?" asked Jack, "My girlfriend's name is Lisa Smith. Gerald is the name of her grandfather. She hasn't seen him since she was a child. He didn't go to her grandmother's funeral."

It was almost as though something or someone had prevented the ring from being stolen that night or sold all this time until the right person came along.

Martin smiled and said, "Well, I think it's found it's rightful owner in that case," as he handed the ring to Jack.

"How much do you want for it?" asked Jack as he took hold of the box.

"Nothing, as it was donated to us," replied Martin, "It's yours. It seems to me that it has been waiting for you to come in and claim it."

"Wow, are you sure? That's really kind of you, thank you. Thank you so much," said Jack elated, eagerly shaking the Martin's hand.

"You're very welcome," smiled Martin, "Take care now."
Jack put the small box in his coat pocket and left the store. He couldn't believe how lucky he was to have been able to find Lisa's grandmother's ring like he did. He was so happy and knew this would make things up to Lisa no end.

Jack had a huge smile on his face as he headed back to his car. Not only was he excited at presenting Lisa with the ring but he was also looking forward to spending the rest of his life with her.

As Jack was driving back down the highway, he could feel himself getting really tired again. The lack of sleep was starting to catch up with him. He unintentionally closed his eyes briefly, just for a second. He quickly awoke again to see a deer standing in the middle of the road. He swerved out of the way to avoid it and slammed on the brakes. Jack sat calming down for a minute as the deer ran off back into the woods. He scratched his head, and breathed a sigh of relief, as he knew he'd had a close call.

Chapter Six

It had been a couple of days since Jack last left the house and he still hadn't slept. The sleep deprivation was slowly turning him into an insomniac. It was Lisa's birthday that day and he was taking a break from writing while he was preparing a special surprise for her. His novel was going really well and the thought of proposing to Lisa that evening was keeping him fighting through the tiredness.

Lisa was on her way home from work while Jack was decorating the house with candles and putting the final touches to her birthday surprise.

Ten minutes later, Lisa walked through the door. The house was in darkness apart from the flickering candlelights strategically placed around the hallway, leading into the kitchen where Jack was laying out the table. She looked at him and smiled.

"Happy birthday, sweetheart," he said, as he put the plates down and went round to give her a hug.

"Thank you," she replied, as she rested her head on his shoulder. They sat down at the table and started their meal. Jack wasn't the best chef in the world but he made it as special as he could for Lisa.

Jack smiled at her across the table and said, "I was in town the other day and went past that jewellers that you were admiring the window of. They had some really beautiful earrings and necklaces."

"Oh right," she replied, unaware of what he was about to do.

"Yeah, I, erm, popped in there and had a look around," he said as he put down his knife and fork and stood up.

He walked round to her and put his hand in his pocket as he knelt down in front of her.

Lisa swallowed hard, as he nervously said, "I've reached a point in my life where everything is coming together and is perfect, except there's one thing missing," taking hold of her hand, "I've been thinking about this for a while now and I finally got the courage

together the other day to do this tonight. Lisa Smith, would you make me the happiest man alive by agreeing to be my wife?"
Lisa wiped a small tear away from her eye.

"Yes, Jack. I would love to. More than anything in the world," she gasped.
A huge smile filled his face as he put the ring on her finger before embracing her. She pulled away and looked happily at the ring. She couldn't stop smiling. This was turning out to be the best birthday she has ever had.

"How did you know to get this one?" she asked surprised.

"You said it reminded you of the one that your grandmother used to have when she was alive," he replied, as he stood up and went to sit back down.

"Yes, it does," she remembered fondly, "Very much so."

"Well, I guess you should know that it is, in fact, the same ring," he confessed.

Lisa looked shocked and said, "How do you know that?"

"The guy in the store told me that an elderly gentleman took the ring in there after his wife had passed away. His name was Gerald Smith," replied Jack.

Lisa was becoming overwhelmed and said, "My grandfather? My god, I haven't seen him since I was a teenager. He'd left Nanna for another woman. I guess her belongings went to him as they were still married when she died."
Jack reached across the table and took hold of her hand, holding it tightly.

"I know," he comforted, "The weirdest thing is though, the tray the ring was originally in was stolen a few nights ago. The guy distinctly remembers it being in there when he closed the store. But the following morning, after the break in, the ring was found locked away in the drawer under the cash register."

"It's almost as though Nanna was protecting it and waiting for you to go in and get it," shuddered Lisa at the thought of her Grandmother's spirit protecting something so materialistic, but what meant so much to her.

"Exactly," replied Jack.

The following morning, Lisa woke up and saw Jack lying next to her wide-awake. He'd been up all night watching her sleep. He had been doing that a lot the last few nights. She looked at him and smiled.

"Good morning. How long have you been awake for?" she asked.

He stroked the side of her cheek.

"I've forgotten now," he smiled back.

"You should really get some sleep, you look so tired, " she insisted.

"I know," he replied, "And I will when I finish the book. I promise. I will sleep forever if that's what makes you happy."

She looked at the clock and saw it said 9.30am. She was already late for work. Leaping out of bed, she hurried to get ready.

"Oh my god! You're not a very good alarm clock are you?" she joked.

Jack laughed and said, "I guess not. I didn't realise what the time was. Sorry, sweetheart."

"That's okay," she said, "I can't stay mad at you anyway. You're too easy to forgive," as she finished getting ready for work.

She walked over to kiss him goodbye.

"I had better go," she said.

"Okay my love," he replied, "I'll see you tonight," before yawning.

"Get that book finished, so you can get some sleep," she said as she left to go to work. Jack smiled and got out of bed. He walked over to his laptop and sat down on the chair. He was determined to finish this book if it was the last thing he ever did.

Chapter Seven

The following day, Jack was deeply engrossed in his latest chapter. He had managed to write nineteen chapters in less than a week. He wished he'd found that kind of inspiration before then perhaps he could already be one of the greatest writers there is and as good as his hero was. But Jack was still young and had his whole life ahead of him. And although the lack of sleep was getting to him, he knew it would be all worth it in the end.

An hour later his phone rang, as he was busy typing away.
"Hello?" he said, answering it.
"G'day mate," said Billy, "How's the story coming along? Is it finished yet?"
Jack laughed.
"No, not yet but it's getting there," he replied enthused, "Couldn't be more pleased with how it's going. I just have a few more chapters left to do. I should be done by the end of this week if I can carry on the way I am."
"Excellent stuff!" said Billy excitedly, "I really can't wait to read it from what you told me about it the other day. The plot line sounded fantastic!"
"Good, I'm really enjoying writing it. So much so I can't bloody stop! I tell you what I'll do if it makes you happy, I'll fax the first few chapters over to you, just to give you an idea of what's to come," suggested Jack.
"That's bonza mate," replied Billy, "I'll look forward to it. Anyway, I'll leave you in peace to carry on, my good friend."
"Cheers, Bill," said Jack, "Speak to you later."
After Jack got off the phone he printed off the first three chapters and wrote a quick covering note to Billy before faxing them off to him.

He walked around the house for a bit, before carrying on with his work.

Later on that day Billy called him back.

"G'day mate, it's Billy again. Just phoning to say that this is excellent!" he said.

"Gee thanks, Bill," replied Jack, "Do you really think so?"

"Of course!" beamed Billy, "Don't take this the wrong way but this is probably the best thing you have ever written, and you know I'm a massive fan of yours anyway. But this is just…well, I'm lost for words!"

"Ah wow, I don't know what to say," said an ecstatic Jack, "That really means a lot."

"No worries, mate. Oh, and I don't care what you say by the way. Jack Somerfield is going on as the author," insisted Billy.

Jack laughed and said, "Whatever you say, Bill."

"So are you going to fax me some more or do I have to wait until the end?" asked Billy.

"You're gonna have to wait till it's finished I'm afraid. I can't be giving away the whole twist of the story, can I?" teased Jack.

"Spoil sport," joked Billy, "Okay I'll let you carry on with the good work then. Speak to you later."

"Yep, speak to you soon," replied Jack as he hung up the phone. The comments from Billy had made his day. He knew it was the best thing he had ever written, but to hear someone else say it was a different matter. It felt like a massive weight had been lifted off of his shoulders. Since he almost crashed on his way back from buying Lisa the ring, he'd been feeling really tense about things. He was worried that maybe what he was writing wasn't as good as he thought it would be and that perhaps he was wasting his time with it all. Now he could relax and enjoy finishing off the rest of his book.

Later that night, Lisa came home after a long shift. Jack was still writing away when she walked through the door.

"So when are you going to let me read this one?" she asked.
He smiled and turned around.

"When it's finished," he replied, "I'm almost done. Be patient. All good things come to those who wait."

She smiled back and said, "I look forward to it. Anyway, I'm going to go to bed as it's been a long day," as she walked over to kiss him goodnight, "Don't stay up too late."

"Okay, honey," he replied as she went to bed, before turning back round to face his laptop.

Chapter Eight

The following morning, Lisa was rudely awoken by the sound of the alarm. She looked over at Jack's side of the bed and noticed that it hadn't been slept in again. She sighed as she got out of bed and went into the study.

"Have you been here all night?" she asked.

"Hmm, I must have been," replied Jack, "I'm sorry, but once I get started in these things, I get so into the story that I lose all sense of time."

"This sleep deprivation can't be doing you any good though. I worry about you sometimes," she commented.

"Ah, don't worry about me. I'll sleep when I'm dead," he replied.

"Don't say things like that!" she snapped, "You know it upsets me to think about those things."

He got up and walked over to her.

Putting his arms around her he said, "Okay, okay, I'm sorry. I won't say it again. I promise."

"You better not," she replied as she put her arms around him.

"You have my undying word," he insisted.

She smiled and said, "Anyway, I guess I should get ready for work."

"Okay then," he sighed, as he let her go, "I guess I better let you go then."

"See you later," she said, as she went to get ready.

"I'll still be here," he replied, as she walked away.

Jack sighed as he heard the door slam behind Lisa as she left the now seemingly empty house. He hated what the lack of sleep was doing to his state of mind and how it was affecting his relationship with Lisa. Despite everything though, he knew he had to finish the book. No matter what was happening in the here and now, this would be their future together. Jack now believed he could do this; that he could make a success out of all the hard work he was putting into it. He sat back down in front of his laptop and carried on typing away.

Jack was on his penultimate chapter. He couldn't believe he was nearly finished. He wasn't even feeling tired anymore. That had passed by a few days ago, as he was just used to being awake now. If anything he was probably running on adrenaline. He knew that he could probably sleep for eternity once he had finished though. It had taken him just seven days to write twenty-eight chapters, and the thirtieth would be his final chapter.

Chapter Nine

Just off Highway 33, by the small village of Wainfleet, a young couple were driving along the Interstate when one of them desperately needed to stop for a bathroom break. There weren't any rest rooms along the way, so they quickly ducked into the bushes by a ditch. They were startled when they came across an overturned car. The man went running back up to his car to where his girlfriend was waiting for him.

"What's wrong?" she asked as he jumped back in the car, reaching for his cellphone.

"It looks like there's been an accident," he said, as he called the emergency services.

Lisa was back at the headquarters when the call came in. She stopped what she was doing and headed out with her partner, Laurie, to the scene.

At the same time the young man called the emergency services, his girlfriend had called her brother at the press office. There had been a string of accidents along the same stretch of road in recent months and the government denied that the roads were in a poor state and were dangerous to drive on. They thought by getting the press involved that that this would make them sit up and take notice, so they could no longer deny that the roads were in dire need of repair.

Jack was starting chapter twenty-nine when he phoned Billy to tell him that he was almost done and would Fed-Ex the manuscript to him this afternoon.

"I can't believe that you've got this all done in a week," said Billy.

"Me neither," laughed Jack, "I can't believe that it's almost over. I've been so engrossed in it that I don't even know what day it is."

Billy laughed back and said, "That's good. It means it will captivate your readers and make you a rich man."
Jack laughed again.

"I just want to be successful though, Bill. That's all I've ever wanted," he said, "Money doesn't bother me that much if I'm honest, as long as I can be as great as the rest of them one day is what matters to me."

"And you will be," said Billy, "I'll see to it. That's a promise. Listen, is there something up with your phone line as I can barely here you?"

"I don't think so, I'm not sure," replied Jack, "Anyway, I'll crack on as I need to finish this."

"No worries, mate," said Billy, "We'll go for a few beers at the weekend to celebrate you finishing."

"Definitely, I'll look forward to it," said Jack, "Speak to you soon."

Lisa and Laurie arrived at the scene of the accident along Highway 33, and went over to the couple to take their statements. As they approached the wreckage, Lisa's cell phone started ringing.

"Hello?" she said as she answered it.

"Hello, sweetheart," said Jack, "I'm just giving you a quick call to let you know that I'm on the final chapter at last. So you can read it when you come home."

"Ah that's great news," she replied, "Then perhaps you can get some sleep."

Jack laughed and said, "Of course I will. I promise."

"Listen, I better go sweetheart as I'm just heading out to a crash site," she said.

"Oh no, I hope the driver is okay," he replied, "I'll see you later then. I love you."

"I love you too," said Lisa, "Bye."

Jack looked at his cell phone and noticed that the battery was now dead. There was also a crack on the screen that he hadn't noticed before.

"That's weird," he said to himself as he put the phone down and carried on writing chapter thirty.

Laurie commented to Lisa as she walked over to the incident, "Hasn't your Jack got a car like this one?"

Lisa looked at the wreckage and said, "Yeah, he has. It's his pride and joy. He bought it with his first payout from Billy. He'd be really gutted if he saw the state of this one. Let's hope he doesn't watch the news later with the vultures out here pecking at any story they can lay their grubby hands on."

"To be fair though, Lisa, it's about time they did something with these roads. How many times have we been called out here?" said Laurie.

"Yeah, true. You have a point," sighed Lisa, "Maybe if they see this it'll make them sit up and think and actually do something about it."

"Here's hoping," said Laurie, "I really don't know how many more families I can break the news to because of it. It's too heartbreaking watching the pain of someone losing a loved one. I couldn't imagine if that happened to me, I don't know how I would cope."

"Same here," agreed Lisa, "I don't think I could go through that level of loss either. Especially when this could be so easily fixed if the government would pull their finger out and do something about the state of these roads."

Jack was coming up to the last paragraph of the final chapter. He logged onto the Fed-Ex website and booked a collection with them to pick up the manuscript for an hours time, giving him just enough time to print off the completed novel and put it together ready for Billy.

Lisa kept looking at the wreckage of the car in the ditch. She couldn't get over how much it looked like the car Jack had parked on the driveway at home. She felt really bad for the poor soul who would still be trapped inside, but had a feeling of content that they had as good a taste in cars as her beloved fiancé.

The camera crew were standing at the side of the road filming the reporter as they talked about the story that would become that evening's breaking news.
In the meantime, the rescue workers were busy cutting through the wreckage to get to any casualties inside.

Lisa and Laurie were taking statements from the couple that found the wreckage as one of the rescue workers called out to say they had found a body.
"Looks like they've been here a few days," he said.
"How long would you say they've been there for?" asked Lisa.
"I'm not sure, maybe three or four days. It's hard to tell without doing an autopsy," he replied.
"Is there any identification on them?" asked Laurie.
The rescue worker, Nick, went through their personal effects and came across a wallet. He pulled it out and looked at the driver's licence inside.

Chapter Ten

Jack printed off his completed book. He was elated that he had finished but sad to some degree that it had come to an end. He had really enjoyed writing the plotlines, developing the characters and creating the final big twist at the end. He knew in his heart that it would be a best seller and he was proud to put his real name on there. Many people would think he was an unknown author, but his real fans would know that Jack Russell was his pen name and Jack Somerfield was the real writer. The last page printed just as there was a ring on the doorbell. He went to answer it with the 175 pages in his hand and saw the Fed-Ex courier standing on his doorstep.

"Hi there, do you have any spare envelopes?" asked Jack, "I'm all out of them."

"Right here, Mr Somerfield," replied the driver, handing one to him.

Jack took the envelope off him and put the finished manuscript inside. He sealed it before writing Billy's details on the front and handing it back to the driver.

"Have a nice day, sir," he smiled as he took it and headed back to his van, driving away.

Jack was now feeling a little lost and didn't know what to do with himself. He didn't know why, but he had the urge to switch on the news.

Back at the crash site, the rescue worker called out the drivers' name.

Billy was sitting in his office watching the news unfold when the Fed-Ex driver turned up with Jack's finished manuscript. He signed for the envelope before trying to call Jack on his cell phone. It went straight through to voicemail.

"Hey buddy," said Billy, "Just got your manuscript and I can't wait to read it. Anyway, I guess you're on the phone to Lisa so give me a call later and we'll arrange a time to meet for these beers at the weekend. Take care, mate."
He hung up the phone and carried on watching the news about the accident along Highway 33.

Jack was standing watching the news, frozen to the spot, as it all started coming back to him.

"The car belongs to a Jack Somerfield," said Nick.
Lisa dropped her notebook and pencil as she dropped to the floor in shock. Laurie looked at her, aghast, and knelt down in front of her.
"Oh my god, Lisa. I'm so sorry," she said as she put her arms around her.
Lisa was speechless. The tears flooded out as she rest her head on Laurie's shoulder.
"I'm so, so sorry," comforted Laurie.
"But it can't be," sobbed Lisa, "It just can't be! Jack's at home! I left him there this morning. He can't be dead! He just can't be!"

Jack sighed as he carried on watching the news. He felt a sense of relief that his body had been found, now he could rest in peace.
He cast his mind back to the day he went to buy Lisa the engagement ring and remembered how he had fallen asleep at the wheel of his car. Then all that was left was darkness. On that fateful day, Jack never woke up again after his car had veered off the road and overturned into a ditch at the side of Highway 33, just outside Wainfleet. The impact had killed him instantly. The last few days were beginning to become a blur to him, as he was starting to fade away. The sheer determination Jack had to finish his book, and the power from Lisa's grandmother's ring, had kept his spirit alive long

enough to do so. Lisa's grandmother had always promised to make sure Lisa had a better life than she had and the opportunity to do the things she never could. She had been watching over Lisa since she died and knowing how talented Jack was, she kept his spirit there so he could complete his work for it to be published and eventually go on to be a best seller, giving her granddaughter financial security from the money made from the sales of his book, his first and final masterpiece.

Lisa looked at the ring on her finger and felt sick.

"But he gave this to me two nights ago," she sobbed, "How can that be him?"

"I don't know," said Laurie, "I really don't know. Do you want me to take you home?"

Lisa shook her head.

"I have to see him," she said, "I have to know if that's really him in the car."

Jack looked around the study one last time before sitting back down at his laptop. The cup of coffee that Lisa had made for him that morning still sat there, half drunk and stone cold.

Nick and the rest of the team had got Jack's body out of the wreckage and was wheeling it towards the back of the coroner's van. Lisa ran over to them before they put him in the back.

"Wait! I want to see him," she cried, "I need to know!"

Laurie closely followed and stood next to her, placing her hand on Lisa's shoulder as they unzipped the body bag.

It was Jack.

Lisa sobbed uncontrollably as her whole world came crashing down around her.

Laurie put her arms around her.

"I'm so, so sorry," she comforted.
Lisa couldn't speak or move, she just kept on crying and shaking.

Jack finished writing Lisa a goodbye letter on the laptop before printing it off. He knew he had overstayed his time but had to do that one last thing. He left it on the printer and stood up. Looking out the window, he saw his car was no longer parked on the drive. He walked towards the front door and disappeared without a trace.

Chapter Eleven

An hour had passed by and Lisa had finally stopped crying as she tried to come to terms with this unwelcome, new reality that had been thrust upon her.

"Are you alright?" asked Laurie as they sat in the patrol car.

Lisa swallowed hard.

"I don't know," she sighed, wiping the tears away from her eyes with a handkerchief that her grandmother had given to her when she was a child after falling off her bike in their back garden. She needed her more than ever now. The fear of being alone was starting to dawn on her.

"Come on, I'll take you home," said Laurie as she started the engine.

"I can't believe he's really dead," sighed Lisa, "I just can't understand it."

"I know, me neither," agreed Laurie, "Jack was a wonderful man who adored you very much."

"But I spoke to him on the phone less than an hour ago," said a confused Lisa, "You were there. He phoned to tell me he had finished his book."

"Maybe that's what he stayed for?" suggested Laurie as she pulled away from the side of the road and headed back to Lisa's home, "Perhaps that's what kept him here, to finish the book."

"He was determined to complete it. I know that, as that's all he would talk about," Lisa swallowed hard, "I don't know what I'm going to do without him."

"At least he can rest now," comforted Laurie, "I know that's not what you want to hear right now but it's true."

Lisa broke down again.

"I don't know if I can face going home," she sobbed, "I can't imagine being without him."

"He's always going to be there, Lisa," insisted Laurie, "He'll always live on in your heart."

They arrived outside within ten minutes. It was hard for Lisa not seeing Jack's car parked on the driveway anymore. As they went inside, the house was empty but Lisa still felt his presence there, giving her a strange sense of relief inside.
Laurie went into the study and saw a piece of paper on the printer. She picked it up and took it back out to the hallway, handing it to Lisa.

"What's this?" asked Lisa, taking hold of the seemingly blank piece of paper.
Laurie shrugged her shoulders.

"I'm not sure," she replied, "I found it on top of the printer."
Lisa flipped over the piece of paper as the words started to appear in a ghostly fashion, she began reading.

To my darling Lisa, I'm so sorry I have to leave you now but it's time for me to go. Just remember that I will always love you and look after you when you need me. I'll forever be in your heart as you will in mine. Take care, my love. Until we meet again, Jack xxx

Chapter Twelve

It was the day of Jack's funeral. Lisa was sitting in the chair Jack had been glued to whilst creating his masterpiece. She looked at the photograph on the desk of the two of them from when they had first got together and smiled as she remembered all the happy times they had spent together.

She had just finished writing his eulogy when the doorbell rang. It was her brother Archie. Lisa opened the door and Archie threw his arms around his little sister.

"How are you doing, sis?" he asked.

"Better, thanks," she replied, "I've been thinking about when we first met."

Archie smiled as he held his sister in his arms.

"Yeah, I remember that too. He was scared of me to start with," he laughed.

Lisa laughed back and said, "That's because you were being too protective of me."

"I was just looking out for you, sis," insisted Archie, "Anyway, it didn't take me long to start trusting him. He was a good lad."

"Yes, he was," sighed Lisa as she started to well up again.

"Sorry," he comforted, "I didn't mean to…"

"It's okay," she said, cutting in, "I know he's gone, bro. But I also know he's here with me."

Archie swallowed hard and said, "I'm going to miss that crazy boy! I was just getting used to having him around."

"If you want, you could say a few words as well," suggested Lisa.

"Thank you," he smiled, "I'd appreciate that very much."

She smiled back as she let him go.

"I guess we should get going," she said.

"I guess so," he replied, picking up her jacket off the back of the chair and putting it over her shoulders.

Billy was sitting on a pew with his girlfriend, Sandra, behind Jack's parents who had flown out from London for the funeral. Billy clutched hold of Sandra's hand when Lisa and Archie walked in through the church doors. Archie went to sit with them as Lisa sat with Jack's parents.

"How's she doing?" whispered Billy.

"It's hard to tell," replied Archie, "She said she's doing better but I never know whether she's telling the truth or not."

"How about you?" asked Sandra.

Archie sighed, "I'm gonna miss him."

Lisa sat down next to Jack's mum.

"It's good to see you, Lisa," said Pauline, as she took hold of her hand, "It's just too bad it's not under different circumstances."

Lisa nodded and said, "I know. But it is good to see you too."

As the service began, Lisa began to realise just how much she was missing Jack. Things were very tough for her but she hadn't told Archie how much she was really hurting. The time had come for her to get up and say her last goodbyes to the man she loved more than life itself.

"I'll never forget the first time I met Jack," she began, "He was over here on business when he came into a bar where I was working part time. It was love at first sight. He'd stay until the early hours of the morning and walk me home afterwards. He was such a gentleman. From that day, we promised to always be together."

Lisa began to well up and struggled to continue. Archie got up out of his seat and walked over to his sister, putting his arms around her.

"Jack was an amazing guy," he said, "From the moment I met him I knew I would have a problem trying to part them. Not that I would have wanted to as I felt happy with Lisa being with him and knew he would look after her. When he went back to the UK, it was hard on all of us as he was such a great lad, but we knew that when the time was right and the good lord helped him along the way, that he would come back to our family," Archie swallowed hard before carrying on, "I just wish I had more time to have got to know him better," looking at the photo on the coffin, "Jack, I'll miss you brother. Until we meet again."

Archie took Lisa by the hand and they went and sat back down for the rest of the service.

Chapter Thirteen

The following weeks after Jack's funeral were hard on everyone. He had touched so many lives and everyone who knew him was now left with a void in their hearts. In this time Billy had been promoting Jack's book that he had been working so hard to get finished and what regrettably was the cause of his untimely demise. Billy and Lisa had discussed thoroughly beforehand whether to go ahead and publish the book but came to an agreement that it should be done in his memory, so the world can see just how talented Jack Somerfield was and what he could have aspired to be.

Lisa had gone down to OzCorp for a de-briefing with Billy. The book was an overnight success and in the first 24 hours had sold out in twenty bookstores across Canada alone and America was struggling to keep up with demand. All the effort Jack had put into writing it and the promotion Billy had been doing was paying off.

"The boy done good," said Billy, "You should be proud of him."

Lisa smiled and said, "I am, very. And though I know he's gone, I can still feel he's with me all the time."

"Me too," replied Billy nodding, "He was quite a character and will always be missed."

Lisa put her hand on her stomach and said, "He'll live on through this one when he or she arrives."

Lisa had recently found out she was pregnant with Jack's child. She was sad that she never got the chance to tell him but comforted knowing that he will always be there with her...in one way or another...

Chapter Fourteen

Ten years later, Luke Somerfield was sitting at his desk at school when his teacher came over to him. Luke was a troubled student and was being bullied by his classmates for not having a father around at sports days and soccer games. Lisa was trying her best to be there for him but was working every hour she could to support them both. The money that was made from the sales of Jack's book was put into a trust fund for Luke; Lisa thought that would be the best thing to do.

"Is everything alright?" asked the teacher.
Luke sighed before looking at the clock.

"Can I wait here until my mom comes to get me please, miss?" he pleaded.

The teacher put her hand on his shoulder and said, "But it's a lovely day outside. Why don't you play with your friends while you wait?"

"They're not my friends, miss," he replied, "They don't like me."

"Don't be silly," she comforted, "How can they not like you?"
Luke sat forward in his chair and put his hands on his desk.

"Because they keep being horrible to me," he replied with tears in his eyes.

"About what?" she asked.

"About my clothes and why my dad isn't around," he sobbed, unable to fight back the tears.
The teacher pulled up a chair and sat beside him.

"I can only imagine how you must be feeling about that," she said, "Losing a parent at any age is a tough thing to go through, but not having the chance to know one at all must be unbearable."

He swallowed hard and said, "I just wish I could have met him, to have known what he was like. My mom tells me all these stories of what he was like as a person. She says I look like him. Sometimes

I think that makes her sadder. I catch her crying sometimes after she looks at a photo album of them when they first got together. Is that my fault? Did I do something wrong?"

"Of course you didn't," sighed the teacher, "She's just remembering the happy times, that's all."

"But why can't she look at me in the eye?" he asked.

The teacher didn't know what to say to that.

Lisa walked in through the classroom door.

"There you are," she sighed with relief, "I've been looking all over for you."

Luke looked up and saw his mom standing there.

"Is everything okay?" asked Lisa, slightly concerned.

"Yes," replied the teacher, "May I have a quick word?"

"Sure," said Lisa, swallowing hard and wondering what the problem may be.

"If you could just wait here, Luke," insisted the teacher, "I'm just going to have a quick chat with your mom."

He nodded as she stood up and walked away with Lisa.

"What's the problem?" asked a concerned Lisa.

"Are you aware that Luke is being bullied?" queried the teacher.

Lisa shook her head.

"I had no idea," she replied, "He's very quiet when I pick him up from school and doesn't talk about his friends much."

"They taunt him about having no father around," informed the teacher.

Lisa sighed, "Why would they do such a thing?"

"Unfortunately children say the most horrible things when someone is different to they are. It could be about anything; size, height, wearing glasses. But in Luke's case, not having a father is the brunt of their insults," the teacher explained.

Lisa sighed and said, "It's not like he can come back, is it?"

"Have you tried talking to Luke?" asked the teacher.

"Many times," huffed Lisa, "But he doesn't listen to me. I can't seem to get through to him. He talks to my brother more than he does me."

"Maybe you could ask him to talk to Luke about it," suggested the teacher.

"I guess I could try," replied Lisa, "It couldn't do any harm after all."

Later that evening Lisa was on the phone to Archie.

"I don't know what to say to him," she said.

"Do you want me to have a word?" asked Archie.

Lisa sighed.

"That would be great if you could," she replied, "Thanks."

"Anything for you sis," he comforted.

It was 3am, when Luke woke up from a bad dream and for the life of him, he could not get back to sleep. He switched on the light and noticed a shadow appearing in the corner of his room. Startled by this, he pulled the covers up to his head and began shaking, as a ghostly figure appeared right before his eyes.

"Don't be afraid, my son," said the ghostly voice.

"Who are you?" asked Luke.

"I am your father," replied a ghostly Jack, "I wish I could be there for you."

Luke sighed and said, "I wish you were here too, dad," as the tears formed in his eyes.

"Don't let the bullies get to you," insisted Jack, "They only do it because they know they can hurt you."

"How did you know?" asked a confused Luke.

"I've been watching over you, son. I'll always be here for you," comforted Jack, "Even though I can't be with you, I will live on in your heart and mind."

"I know," sighed Luke.

"I have to go know," said Jack, "Do me a favour though before I go."

"Anything," promised Luke.

"Look after your mom for me," pleaded Jack, "You're the man of the house now."

"I will," Luke insisted, "I promise, dad."

"I love you, son," said Jack, as his ghostly figure began to disappear.

"I love you too, dad," yawned Luke, as he drifted off back to sleep.

Chapter Fifteen

The following morning, Luke went charging down the stairs. Lisa was in the kitchen making breakfast when he came running in.

"Slow down!" she said, putting some cereal down on the table, "What are you so bouncy for this morning?"

"I saw dad last night," he replied, smiling, as he sat down at the table.

"Excuse me?" exclaimed Lisa, taken aback by this comment, "What do you mean you saw your dad last night?"

"He told me I was the man of the house now," he smiled, eating his breakfast.

Lisa stopped what she was doing and sat down opposite him.

"Luke, now this is very important. I need you to tell me the truth, and I promise not to get angry," she insisted, "You're not lying to me are you?"

"No, mom," he replied as he heard the school bus pull up outside, "Gotta run!" before kissing her on the cheek and running out of the front door.

Lisa sat glued to the chair at the kitchen table for the next hour or so, frozen. She couldn't move from there, her whole body felt numb. She felt so confused and hurt. Why would Luke make up that sort of story knowing how much she still thinks of Jack everyday? When she finally managed to compose herself, the only thing she could think of doing was to call Archie.

"Hello?" he said, answering the phone tiredly.

"Hi, bro," she replied, still shaken up, "Can you come round this afternoon please?"

"Sure," he yawned, sitting up in bed, "What's wrong? You don't sound yourself."

"It's Luke," she sighed, "I don't know how much more I can take. He's now saying he's seen Jack."

"Sorry? Say that again," said Archie aghast, "What do you mean he's saying he's seen Jack?"

"Exactly what I said," she replied, "He came down this morning and told me he saw his dad last night."
Archie swallowed hard.

"Okay, I'll be round before he finishes school to have a word with him," he insisted, "Just try not to think about it. I know that's difficult to do."

"Thanks, Archie," she sighed, "I'll try to concentrate on these reports I have to finish for work. See you later."

Later that morning, Luke was sitting at the back of the classroom in his usual chair when the bullies came over to taunt him.

"You're in my seat, freak!" one of them said.

Luke looked up and smiled, "I think your place is in the corner of the room with a D hat on your head," he said.
The three bullies walked away with their heads hung in shame.
The teacher looked up and smiled when she heard Luke stand up for himself. He looked over at her and smiled when he realised she was proud of him for what he said. He thought back to his dream last night about Jack and it gave him a glowing sense of confidence. If he could keep that thought with him all the time, he knew the bullies would never be able to scare him again.

Archie arrived at Lisa's house later that afternoon. He rang the doorbell and she came to answer it.

"How are you doing, sis?" he asked, throwing his arms around her.

"Still confused," she replied, "Why would he say this?"

"I don't know," replied Archie, "I wish I knew what was going through his head."

"I'm glad he has you to talk to though. Without a father around, you've kind of taken on that role as his uncle," thanked Lisa.

He let her go and they went into the house.

"I'd be proud if he was my son," insisted Archie, "You've done a great job."

"Thank you," she smiled, taking him by the hand, "Can I get you a drink?"

"I'd love a coffee," he replied, as they went into the kitchen.

An hour later, Luke came in through the front door.

"Hi, mom," he called, as he hung his coat up on the peg.

She came out into the hallway to give him a hug.

"Hi, Luke. How was school today?" she asked.

"It was good," he replied, joyfully, "I stood up to the bullies and the teacher was proud of me for it."

Lisa smiled.

"That's brilliant!" she smiled, "Let's hope they leave you alone from now on."

"They will," he grinned, "All the time I have dad watching over me."

She swallowed hard and quickly changed the subject.

"Uncle Archie's in the kitchen. He's come round to say hello," she said.

Luke's face lit up.

"Great! I'll go and see if he want to play the computer with me," he replied, walking away.

Lisa looked down at the floor and sighed.

"Uncle Archie!" yelled Luke, as he went running into the kitchen and throwing his arms around him.

"Hey, buddy!" replied Archie, hugging him back, "I've missed you."

"Me too," sighed Luke, as he sat on his uncle's lap, almost crushing his legs.

"Blimey!" gasped Archie, feeling the weight of a ten year old on him, "What's your mom been feeding you?"

Luke laughed and asked if he had come round to play the computer with him.

"Not just yet," said Archie, "Sit down a sec...just not on me."

"What is it, uncle Archie? You have your serious face on," asked Luke.

Archie sighed.

"Your mom told me what you said to her this morning about your dad," he said.

"I know! It's great, isn't it?" smiled Luke as he sat down on the chair opposite him.

"No Luke, it's not great. Why would you say something like that?" questioned Archie.

"Don't you believe me?" asked Luke, "I wouldn't lie, you know that!"

Archie sighed. Luke was right, he wouldn't lie about something like that.

"So tell me exactly what happened," he requested.

"I had trouble sleeping because of my latest run in with those horrible kids at school and was trying to come up with a way of getting out of going in the next day. Then something happened. I got very scared as a shadow appeared in the corner of my room and started to talk to me," replied Luke.

"What did he say?" asked Archie, starting to believe him.

"He told me he was my father and not to be afraid anymore. He said that the bullies were only hurting me because they knew they could. I asked him how he knew and he told me that he was watching over me," smiled Luke, "He then told me I was the man of the house now and to look after mom."

Archie swallowed hard as he started to well up. Lisa had been standing at the doorway, listening to everything they were talking about. She walked over to the table in floods of tears, crouching down in front of Luke.

"That sounds like Jack to me," said Archie, before putting his hand on Lisa's shoulder.

She looked round at him and nodded in agreement.

"I know," she sighed, "That is exactly the sort of thing he would have said."

"So was that my dad?" asked Luke.

She took hold of his hands.

"Yes, Luke, it was," she replied, "He was a very amazing man and I know he is watching over us now."

"I can feel him," insisted Luke, "Ever since he came to me last night he's helping me to stand up for myself and have confidence."

Lisa threw her arms around him and held him tightly.

Archie sat back and watched them, as he knew Luke's encounter with Jack had brought him and Lisa closer together. He looked over at the pictures on the wall and noticed something he had never seen before. He stood up and walked over to them, wiping across what he thought was a smudge until he realised it wouldn't disappear. All of the photos of Luke growing up and also the ones of Lisa had a shadow in them nearby. He looked at the picture of Jack and saw a light flicker on his eye, like he was winking. He then smiled when he realised that the shadow in the pictures were Jack and he had been with them all these years and the 'wink' was his way of letting Archie know he will always be with them…

Also available from www.lulu.com and other online retailers…

The Forensic Killer

San Francisco wakes to the news of another brutal killing. The Criminal Investigation Team was baffled by the lack of evidence at this latest crime scene. Just like any other it's the same - no DNA, no evidence, no trace, nothing to implicate a potential suspect.

Victor Corelli heads up the team and had just signed up Tom Johnson as the newest recruit. Young and enthusiastic, Tom has always wanted to be a real hero.

As the lack of evidence brings them no suspects and the bodies begin to pile up, the team are under pressure to find their guy and begin to look a little closer to home. What does it take to catch a killer? As they say it takes one to know one.